I0748251

URBAN HUNT

Laura Shenton

URBAN HUNT

Laura Shenton

Iridescent Toad Publishing

Iridescent Toad Publishing.

©Laura Shenton 2026
All rights reserved.

Laura Shenton asserts the moral right to be identified as the author of this work.

No part of this publication may be
reproduced, stored or transmitted in any form or by any means, electronic, mechanical, photocopying, recording, scanning, or otherwise without written permission from the publisher. It is illegal to copy this book, post it to a website, or distribute it by any other means without permission.

This book is entirely a work of fiction. The names, characters and incidents portrayed in it are the work of the author's imagination. Any resemblance to actual persons, living or dead, events or localities is entirely coincidental.

Designations used by companies to distinguish their products are often claimed as trademarks. All brand names and product names used in this book and on its cover are trade names, service marks, trademarks and registered trademarks of their respective owners. The publishers and the book are not associated with any product or vendor mentioned in this book. None of the companies referenced within the book have endorsed the book.

Cover by Janina Cover Designs.

First edition. ISBN 978-1-913779-99-3

Chapter One

The demon's blood had already started to congeal on Lianne's blade by the time she wiped it clean on the creature's torn jacket. The viscous black substance clung to the silver-edged steel like tar, leaving dark streaks that caught the city lights streaming through the penthouse's floor-to-ceiling windows. Three grand for a possession case wasn't bad money, especially when the client had been stupid enough – or stubborn enough in his denial – to let the thing nest in his penthouse for two weeks before calling her. Easy pickings – a straightforward job that paid the bills.

She slid the curved dagger back into its leather sheath at her thigh, the familiar weight settling against her leg like an old friend. The blade was one of her favourites – perfectly balanced and sharp enough to slice through both flesh and the ethereal substance that demons wore like skin. She'd had it custom-forged by a weaponsmith who specialised in gear for her particular line of work. Her arsenal was certainly formidable: knives, stakes, holy water, and half a dozen other instruments distributed across her body in a configuration that had taken years to perfect.

A shattered mirror on the wall caught her reflection – long, dark hair with a distinctive fringe that framed intense eyes accustomed to spotting the inhuman lurking beneath the human disguise. Her combat-ready attire – a fitted leather top with strategic cut-outs that never hindered movement – had been chosen for function over fashion, though the short flared skirt over armoured leggings had proven practical for concealing an array of weapons. The leather cuffs at her wrists held smaller tools of her trade, each one useful for survival in a world where most people never glimpsed the monsters hiding in plain sight. Everything about her appearance had been honed for her profession – intimidating enough to command respect, yet conventional enough to move through the city without drawing unwanted attention.

Surveying the wreckage of what had once been an expensive living room, Lianne couldn't help but appreciate the demon's thoroughness in destruction. Shattered glass from a crystal chandelier crunched under her boots as she stepped over the overturned coffee table, its marble top split clean in half as if struck by lightning. The modern furniture – all clean lines and designer labels – lay scattered like toys thrown by an angry child. Abstract paintings hung askew on walls that bore deep gouges from claws, their expensive frames cracked and splintered.

The floor-to-ceiling windows that dominated the eastern wall offered a spectacular view of the glittering skyline, the city spreading out below like a circuit board etched in light. Twelve stories up, the sounds of traffic were reduced to a distant hum, and the people moving along the pavements far below looked like ants navigating their concrete maze. One massive pane now sported a spider web of cracks radiating out from a central impact point where the demon had charged in panic, apparently forgetting that twelve floors was a long way down.

"Ms Cross?" The client – some tech billionaire

whose name she'd already forgotten, though his deposit cheque had cleared just fine – hovered near the doorway like he was afraid to enter his own home. His designer suit was rumpled and stained with sweat, his usually perfect hair dishevelled from running his hands through it repeatedly. The confident executive who'd hired her three hours ago had been replaced by a man who looked like he'd aged a decade in a single night. "Is it... is it over?"

Lianne pulled out her phone and snapped several photos of the black ichor staining his white leather sofa, the dark substance eating through the expensive upholstery like acid. Proof of termination for her records – evidence to assure new clients they'd get their money's worth.

"Yeah, it's dead," she said, tucking the phone back into her jacket pocket. "You can come back in." She paused, studying the man's pale face and the way his hands trembled as he fumbled with his tie. "Though you might want to get new furniture."

Or a new penthouse. The sulphur smell would linger for months, a constant reminder of what had happened here. Some clients tried to tough it out, convinced they could live with the aftermath. Most ended up moving within a week, unable to sleep in a place where they'd seen their reality turned inside out.

He nodded frantically, already pulling out his wallet with hands that shook slightly. "Of course, of course. The fee was three thousand, correct?" His voice carried the slight tremor of someone trying very hard to maintain their composure while their worldview crumbled around them. Three hours ago, he'd been a rational man who believed in quarterly reports and market projections. Now he was someone who knew that monsters were real and that they could walk into a person's home wearing their neighbour's face.

"Plus clean-up costs." She gestured at the destroyed room, mentally calculating the damage. The chandelier alone had probably cost more than most people made in a year. "Call it four."

The man didn't even blink as he counted out the bills, his fingers moving automatically through the familiar ritual of payment. Lianne had learnt long ago that the wealthy would pay anything to make their supernatural problems disappear quietly. No police reports, no questions asked, no messy explanations about why their living room looked like a tornado had hit it. They lived in a world where money could solve any problem, and they were willing to pay premium rates to keep it that way.

The crisp hundreds felt substantial in her hands as she folded them into the pocket concealed beneath her skirt, where they joined a small collection of business cards from other clients who'd found themselves in similar situations. Word of mouth was the best advertising in her line of work – satisfied customers who whispered recommendations to other members of their exclusive clubs, always careful to frame it as a joke or urban legend until the moment they found themselves dialling her number at three in the morning.

Just then, her phone buzzed with a text from an unknown number: *Need to talk. Meet me at Café Luna on Fifth. Come alone. – M.*

Lianne frowned, studying the message. The initial 'M' didn't ring any bells, and the tone of the message suggested someone who expected to be taken seriously.

Still, mysterious contacts usually meant money. And money was the reason she got up every morning, the driving force that kept her moving through a job that most people would consider a fast track to an early grave. She'd been hunting demons and their ilk for the better part of a decade, and in that time she'd learnt that survival depended on two things: being very good at what she did, and charging enough to make the risks worthwhile.

Chapter Two

Twenty minutes later, Lianne was sliding into a corner booth at Café Luna, a twenty-four-hour diner that catered to the city's night-shift workers and insomniacs. The place was a relic from a different era, all red vinyl booths and checked linoleum floors, with the kind of atmosphere that spoke of countless stories shared over coffee and pie at ungodly hours. Fluorescent lights hummed overhead, casting everything in a harsh glare that made everyone look slightly ill, while the smell of coffee and bacon grease provided a comforting contrast to the sulphuric stench of demon she'd left behind in the penthouse.

The diner existed in the spaces between the city's more glamorous establishments, serving the people who kept the metropolis running while everyone else slept. Cab drivers grabbing a quick meal between fares, hospital workers coming off the night shift, security guards with a few minutes to kill before making their rounds – all of them united by the shared understanding that the city never truly rested, that there was always someone working while the rest of the world dreamed.

Lianne had barely ordered her coffee – black, no sugar, the kind of utilitarian fuel that had kept her going through more all-nighters than she cared to count – when she felt it. A cold prickle at the base of her neck that made her hand drift instinctively towards her blade, the sensation she'd learnt to associate with things that weren't entirely human. The air itself seemed to thicken, taking on a weight and texture that had nothing to do with the diner's ancient ventilation system.

"You must be Lianne Cross."

The woman who slid into the opposite seat was striking in an otherworldly way that made Lianne's professional instincts sit up and take notice. Pale skin that seemed to glow under the diner's harsh fluorescent lights, as if lit from within by some internal source of illumination. White-blonde hair that moved like it was underwater, defying the stillness of the air around them with subtle currents that suggested depths hidden beneath the surface. Eyes the colour of storm clouds – grey and silver and full of distant thunder.

She wore a black leather jacket over ripped jeans, the kind of carefully curated casual look that probably cost more than most people's rent, but there was something about her presence that made the air itself feel heavier. The conversations at nearby tables seemed to grow quieter, as if the other patrons unconsciously sensed that something dangerous had entered their sanctuary.

"Depends who's asking." Lianne kept her voice neutral, though her fingers remained near her weapon. Years of experience had taught her to trust her instincts, and right now they were screaming that the woman across from her was anything but human. "You're M?"

"Mien." The woman's smile revealed teeth that were too white, too sharp. "And before you reach for that pretty little knife of yours, I should mention I'm not here to fight. I need your help."

"What kind of help?" Lianne asked warily.

"The expensive kind." Mien leaned back in the booth, studying Lianne with an unsettling intensity. Her gaze seemed to catalogue every weapon, every scar, every detail that might prove useful or dangerous. "I need a demon hunter. Specifically, I need you."

Lianne raised an eyebrow, automatically calculating the potential profit against the obvious risk. Specific requests usually came with specific complications, and complications had a way of driving up both the price and the body count. "Flattering, but I don't work with... what are you, exactly?"

"Banshee." Mien said it like she was ordering a sandwich, casual and matter-of-fact, as if admitting to being a harbinger of death was the most natural thing in the world. "And I know what you're thinking – why would a banshee need help killing a demon? Trust me, the irony isn't lost on me either."

Despite herself, Lianne was intrigued. Banshees were rare in the city, most preferring rural areas where their particular brand of supernatural drama played better with the locals. They were creatures of mist and moor, more at home among ancient stone circles than glass towers. This one, though, seemed perfectly at home in the urban jungle, as comfortable in the fluorescent-lit diner as on a windswept hillside.

"I'm listening."

Mien's expression grew serious, the playful edge disappearing from her features. "There's this demon. It's been feeding on the homeless population for months, growing stronger with each kill. The police think it's just another serial killer, but you and I know better."

The mention of missing homeless people sparked a memory – scattered reports in the local news, the kind of stories that got buried on page six because nobody with influence cared enough to demand answers. Bodies found in alleys and abandoned buildings, always with injuries that couldn't quite be explained by conventional means. The police had been spinning theories – copycat killers, gang initiation rituals – anything that better suited their comfortable understanding of urban violence.

"So kill it yourself. Banshees are hardly defenceless."

"This one's different." Mien's fingers drummed against the table, a nervous habit that seemed oddly human given her supernatural nature. The gesture created a soft rhythm against the chipped formica, like raindrops on a window. "It knows I'm coming. Every time I get close, it disappears. I need the element of surprise. They won't expect a banshee to be working with a hunter."

Lianne sipped her coffee, thinking through the implications. Partnership jobs were always messy, more hassle than they were worth.

"What's your stake in this?" she asked finally. "Banshees don't usually play superhero."

Mien's laugh was bitter, seeming to carry echoes of something that went beyond frustration – pain, perhaps. "Let's just say this particular demon and I have history. Bad history." Her eyes flashed with something dangerous, a glimpse of the power that lay beneath her more acceptable façade. "I want it dead, and I'm willing to pay handsomely for the privilege."

"How handsomely?"

"Twenty thousand. Cash."

Lianne nearly choked on her coffee, the bitter liquid burning her throat as she struggled to maintain her composure. Twenty grand was more than she made in two months of regular hunting, the kind of money that could pay for new equipment, better weapons, maybe even a holiday somewhere warm where the most dangerous thing she'd have to worry about was sunburn. Either this banshee was desperate, or the demon was worse than she was letting on. Maybe both.

"What aren't you telling me?"

Mien was quiet for a long moment, staring out the window at the city lights that painted the glass in shifting patterns of gold and white. The silence stretched between them, filled with the ambient noise of the diner – conversations at other tables, the hiss of the coffee machine, the distant sound of traffic that never truly stopped in a city that never slept.

When she spoke, her voice was softer, more vulnerable than before, as if admitting weakness was a luxury she rarely allowed herself. "The demon killed someone I cared about. Someone who didn't deserve to die. And now it's doing the same thing to others, over and over, because that's what feeds it. Not just death – suffering. Prolonged, agonising suffering."

Lianne had seen enough in her line of work to recognise genuine pain when she heard it. The careful control in Mien's voice, the way she held herself just a little too straight, the flash of something raw in her storm-coloured eyes – all of it spoke to a wound that hadn't healed, might never heal. Whatever this was about, it was personal for Mien, which could make her either the perfect partner or a dangerous liability.

Personal vendettas had a way of clouding judgment, making people take risks they normally wouldn't consider. But they also provided motivation that money couldn't match, the kind of driving force that could push someone beyond their usual limitations when the situation demanded it.

"I'll need details. Everything you know about this thing."

Mien smiled, and for the first time, it reached her eyes, transforming her face into something that was genuinely beautiful rather than merely striking. "I was hoping you'd say that."

Chapter Three

The warehouse district at three in the morning was exactly as depressing as Lianne had expected, perhaps more so under the sickly glow of sodium streetlights that had seen better decades. Broken fixtures cast uneven pools of orange light between abandoned buildings, creating a patchwork of illumination and shadow that seemed designed to hide predators. The air carried the lingering scent of industrial decay – rust and old motor oil, concrete dust and chemical residue – mixed with something almost intolerable that made her nose wrinkle and her hand drift instinctively closer to her weapons.

This part of the city had been left behind by progress, a forgotten corner where the urban renewal projects had never reached and the legitimate businesses had long since fled to cleaner, safer districts. Empty lots stretched between crumbling structures, filled with weeds that pushed through cracked asphalt and the rusted remains of machinery that had been abandoned when the last factory closed its doors. The silence was oppressive, broken only by the distant hum of traffic from the main roads and the occasional skitter of rats through the debris.

"Charming place," Lianne muttered.

Mien walked beside her with unsettling silence, seeming to step out of the shadows themselves as if darkness was simply another doorway she could use at will. The banshee moved with fluid grace that spoke of supernatural reflexes, her footsteps making no sound on the broken pavement despite the steel-toed boots she wore. There was something predatory about the way she carried herself, like a wolf pretending to be a dog until the moment came to bare its fangs.

"The demon's been using the old Meridian Steel plant as its base," she said, pointing towards a cluster of rusted smokestacks silhouetted against the sky like skeletal fingers clawing at the stars. "Three blocks that way. It drags its victims there to... play with them."

The smokestacks rose from a complex of industrial buildings that had once employed half the neighbourhood, back when this part of the city had been the beating heart of high-demand manufacturing. Now they stood empty and corroding, monuments to an economic collapse that had turned thriving communities into urban wastelands. The perfect place for something that preferred to do its work away from prying eyes.

They'd spent the previous day planning their approach, holed up in Lianne's apartment while Mien spread maps and photographs across the kitchen table like a general preparing for war. Normally, Lianne preferred not to bring anyone into her home – it was a private space, her sanctuary. But knowing the pitfalls of working with another, and being so used to hunting alone, she'd decided to take the risk this time; this kind of teamwork required a level of planning and discretion that simply couldn't be done in public.

Lianne had been surprised by how methodical Mien could be when she focused, her earlier emotional vulnerability replaced by cold, calculating precision. The banshee had mapped out the demon's hunting patterns with the thoroughness of a forensic investigator, identified its preferred victim types through careful analysis of police reports and missing person files, and had even tracked down city records showing the plant's layout from the municipal archives.

Whatever else she was, she wasn't stupid. That was reassuring – a stupid partner was a quick way to get killed in this business.

Lianne checked her gear one final time, running through the familiar ritual that had become second nature over the years. Silver-edged blades, holy water in reinforced glass vials, a few other tricks of the trade she'd picked up during her travels. Iron filings in small pouches, consecrated salt in waterproof containers, and the small silver cross her grandmother had given her – more for luck than protection, but old habits died hard.

"I'm certain it's a grief demon," Mien said, her voice adopting the clinical tone she'd used during their planning session. "Powerful. Dangerous. It feeds on emotional trauma – specifically, the kind that comes from forcing someone to watch a loved one die slowly and horribly." Her voice was steady, but Lianne caught the slight tremor beneath the words, the carefully controlled emotion threatening to break through her composure. "The longer the suffering, the more prolonged the agony of its victims, the stronger it gets."

The description sent a chill down Lianne's spine. Most demons were content with quick kills, feeding on death itself rather than the complex emotions that surrounded it. A creature that could sustain itself on psychological torture was something else entirely – patient, intelligent, and utterly without mercy.

"Your theory is plausible, but what makes you so sure?"

Mien was quiet for several steps, her boots making no sound on the broken glass and scattered debris as they made their way deeper into the abandoned district. The silence stretched between them, filled with the distant sounds of the city that never truly slept – sirens in the distance, the rumble of late-night delivery trucks, the occasional shout from some street corner drama playing out blocks away.

When Mien finally answered, her voice was softer, more vulnerable than Lianne had heard it before. "My sister. Elena. She was... human. Completely, utterly human – without a trace of supernatural blood in her veins. She was dating some lowlife who got mixed up with the wrong crowd, owed money to the wrong people. Gambling debt that spiralled out of control – the kind of stupid mistakes desperate people make when they think they can solve their problems with one big score." The pain in Mien's voice was unmistakable now – raw and unhealed despite the months that had passed. "They used the demon to make an example of him."

Lianne stopped walking, turning to study the banshee's face in the uncertain light. "They summoned it deliberately?"

"Small-time gangsters who thought they were being clever," Mien continued, her pale, slender hands clenching into fists at her sides. "They wanted to send a message to other debtors, make the guy's death memorable enough that word would spread through the community. So they called up something that specialises in prolonged agony, something that could make death last for days instead of minutes." Her voice grew colder, more controlled, but Lianne could see the fury burning in her eyes. "Elena was with him when it happened. She'd gone to his apartment to try to talk him into getting help, maybe convince him to come clean to his family about the debt. The demon... it made her watch. Every second of it. Every scream, every plea for mercy, every moment of Danny's slow, horrible death. And when it was done with him, when there was nothing left but his corpse and madness in the air, it decided she was next."

Lianne had seen plenty of supernatural cruelty in her time, had witnessed atrocities that would haunt most people's nightmares for the rest of their lives, but this was beyond the usual demon methodology. Most evil spirits were opportunistic predators, feeding when the chance presented itself. This creature was calculating and sadistic.

"I'm so sorry," she said finally, meaning every word. "When did it happen?"

"Six months, two weeks, and three days ago." The precision of Mien's answer belonged to someone who had been counting every moment since her loss. "I've been after it ever since, tracking its movements through the city's underground, following the trail of bodies it leaves behind. It has learnt to recognise my presence. Every time I get close, it bolts, disappears into whatever hellish dimension these things call home." A razor-sharp smile slowly crept onto Mien's face, predatory and eager. "But it won't expect you; hunters are a different kind of threat entirely."

They reached the plant's perimeter fence, a barrier of twisted metal topped with razor wire that had seen better days. Rust had eaten through the steel in places, leaving jagged holes from years of neglect and decay. Warning signs hung at irregular intervals, their paint faded and peeling, proclaiming the dangers of trespassing on private property in multiple languages. Not that anyone with legitimate business would have reason to be here at this hour.

Mien produced a pair of heavy-duty bolt cutters from somewhere in her jacket and made short work of the chain holding the gate closed. The metal parted with a sharp snap that seemed unnaturally loud in the industrial silence, and the gate swung open with a protesting squeal of hinges that hadn't been oiled in years.

"Question," Lianne said as they slipped through the gap, automatically scanning their surroundings for signs of surveillance or security measures. "If this thing killed your sister six months ago, why is it still here? Most demons feed and move on, following opportunities rather than establishing permanent territories."

"Because it's found the perfect hunting ground." Mien gestured at the abandoned buildings around them, empty structures that had once housed hundreds of workers and now served as shelter for society's most vulnerable. "Homeless camps in the steam tunnels, drug addicts shooting up in the old break rooms, prostitutes bringing clients to places where no one will hear them scream. People no one will miss or look for. It can take its time with each victim, savouring the experience."

The insight was as disturbing as it was logical. The demon had found a reliable way to feed on human suffering that could sustain it indefinitely. No wonder it had stayed in one place – why abandon paradise to hunt in less fertile grounds?

The plant's main building loomed ahead of them. Five stories of brick and steel that had once hummed with the sounds of productivity now stood silent and hollow, broken windows staring down like dead eyes that had witnessed too much. Graffiti covered the lower walls in violent splashes of colour – gang tags and artistic statements, political slogans and simple profanity, all layered over each other in a chaotic collage of urban decay.

Somewhere in the distance, metal creaked in the wind, a rhythmic complaint that provided an eerie soundtrack to their approach. The sound seemed to come from everywhere and nowhere, as if the building itself was groaning under the weight of accumulated misery.

"These motion sensors are ancient," Lianne said, studying the entrance with professional interest. "There's no way they still work."

"That's right," Mien replied. "If they looked even remotely functional, I'd have disabled them when I scouted the area. I may be impulsive, but I'm not suicidal. Still, I figured it was worth investing in a bit of tech tailored to our needs." She pulled out what looked like a modified smartphone, equipped with unfamiliar sensors and attachments. With practiced ease, she manipulated the device, its screen displaying a thermal overlay of the structure ahead. "Three heat signatures on the third floor. Two human, one definitely not."

The technology impressed Lianne despite herself. Most supernatural beings were surprisingly low-tech, relying on instinct and tradition rather than modern tools. Mien's willingness to embrace technology suggested a pragmatic approach to hunting that would, hopefully, bode well for their partnership.

Lianne felt the familiar pre-hunt tension settle into her muscles, that combination of anticipation and controlled fear that had kept her alive through a long history of encounters with things that wanted to kill her. This was the part she lived for, the moment when all the planning and preparation crystallised into action, when theory became practice and survival depended on split-second decisions and perfectly executed techniques.

"How do you want to play this?"

"You go in loud," Mien said, her own body language shifting into readiness. "Make it think you're just an amateur looking for a quick score, maybe following up on rumours about something dangerous in the area. I'll circle around through the lower levels, cut off its escape routes before moving into position." Her eyes glowed faintly in the darkness, reflecting available light like those of a nocturnal predator. "When it runs – and it will run – I'll be waiting."

They split up at the entrance, Mien vanishing into the shadows with unnatural stealth while Lianne made her way towards the main stairwell. The banshee seemed to melt into the darkness as if it welcomed her, her pale form becoming indistinct until she was nothing more than a whisper of movement that might have been a trick of the light.

Lianne deliberately let her boots echo on the concrete steps as she climbed, announcing her presence to anything listening. The stairwell was a study in institutional decay, its walls stained with decades of moisture damage and the occasional splash of graffiti. Emergency lighting fixtures hung dark and useless, their plastic covers cracked and yellowed with age. The handrail glistened with a sticky residue she deliberately avoided touching, choosing instead to keep her hands to herself as she climbed. Each step produced echoes that seemed to stretch on forever in the building's hollow interior.

The third floor reeked of mould and something worse – the psychic residue of prolonged suffering that clung to places where horrible things had happened repeatedly. Lianne had encountered it before in places where demons had fed extensively, a kind of spiritual stain that made the air itself feel thick and oppressive, as if the very atmosphere had been poisoned by accumulated anguish. It was the smell of despair made manifest, fear given physical form that invaded her lungs and made her skin crawl with sympathetic horror.

She found the first victim in what had once been a supervisor's office, the kind of glass-walled space that had allowed middle management to keep an eye on the factory floor while maintaining the illusion of executive privilege. The furniture had long since been stripped away by scavengers, leaving only the basic infrastructure and a metal chair that looked like it had been bolted to the floor specifically for the demon's purposes.

For a moment, she thought he was dead.

Then he moved – just barely.

He was male, mid-thirties, slumped and bound to the chair with lengths of barbed wire twisted into patterns that showed not only restraint but also his captor's intent to make him suffer. The wire had been positioned to cause maximum pain without causing injuries that might prove immediately fatal.

His eyes tracked her with a flicker of desperate hope – the kind that belonged to someone who had stopped expecting rescue but hadn't quite let go of the possibility. His clothes hung in tatters, stained with blood and worse, and the stench of infection clung to him in waves, a warning that some of his wounds had been left to fester.

"Please," he whispered through cracked lips, dry enough to suggest a long time without water. "It's been... days..."

Lianne's jaw tightened as she took in the full scope of the demon's handiwork. This wasn't random violence or opportunistic feeding – this was art, if art could be made from human suffering.

Grief demons were particularly sadistic even by supernatural standards, keeping their victims alive for as long as possible to maximise the emotional trauma they could harvest from the experience. They fed not just on death but on the entire spectrum of human suffering: fear, despair, hopelessness – and the special agony that came from watching another endure unimaginable pain.

She crouched beside the man, checking his restraints. "I'm going to get you out of here," she said quietly, pulling out a knife to cut the wires. "But I need you to stay quiet, understand?"

He nodded weakly, his eyes bright with tears of relief he probably didn't have the fluid reserves to spare. She began carefully slicing through his bonds, taking care to avoid the barbed points that had been twisted into his flesh. The wire had cut deep, leaving angry red welts across his wrists and chest, but there was hope he would live if they could get him medical attention soon.

A faint sniffling caught Lianne's attention – soft, almost childlike, and coming from the room next door. She glanced at the man, ensuring he was stable for the moment, then rose to her feet and crossed the threshold into the adjacent office with quiet urgency.

The second victim was in worse shape – an elderly woman who appeared to be unconscious, though her pulse was steady when Lianne checked it. She'd been bound to a similar chair with the same methodical cruelty, but her injuries suggested she'd been here longer, subjected to more of the demon's attention. Her breathing was shallow but consistent, and Lianne made the tactical decision to prioritise evacuation over immediate first aid.

"How touching."

The voice came from behind her, cultured and amused, with the kind of refined accent that suggested education and a lifetime of privilege. Lianne spun around to find the demon watching her from the doorway.

Despite her years of experience hunting its kind, she felt her breath catch.

It had taken the form of a middle-aged businessman, the kind of perfectly groomed executive who populated the city's financial district during business hours. Its expensive suit somehow remained pristine despite the squalid surroundings, the silk tie knotted with mathematical precision, and the Italian leather shoes gleaming. Even its hair was styled with exactness, the kind of no-nonsense cut popular among high-powered businessmen.

Only its eyes gave it away – solid black orbs that reflected the dim light like oil slicks, completely devoid of the warmth or humanity that animated a truly human face. They were the eyes of something that had never been human, had never understood concepts like empathy or mercy except as weaknesses to be manipulated.

"A hunter," it said conversationally, stepping into the room with the casual confidence of something that had never encountered a threat it couldn't handle. "How delightfully predictable. Though I must say, your timing is impeccable. I was just about to begin the evening's entertainment."

The demon's presence filled the room like a physical weight, oppressive and suffocating in a way that had nothing to do with the building's poor ventilation. This was power made manifest, the kind of supernatural force that could bend reality to its will through sheer malevolent intent. Lianne could feel it pressing against her consciousness, testing her mental defences, looking for psychological vulnerabilities it could exploit.

She rolled her shoulders back slowly, her hand moving to the curved blade at her hip with the kind of deliberate care that revealed she understood exactly how dangerous the situation had become. "Sorry to disappoint, but the show's over."

The demon's laughter reverberated from impossible angles, as if the very walls themselves were mocking her. "Oh, my dear girl... the show has only just begun."

Chapter Four

The demon moved faster than Lianne had expected, its businessman façade dissolving into something far more dangerous as it crossed the room in a blur of motion that defied physics. Its form seemed to bend the air around it, creating distortions that made tracking its movement nearly impossible. She threw herself sideways, feeling the displaced air from its grasping claws brush against her cheek like the wing of some massive, predatory bird.

Where its fingers had been, reality seemed to warp slightly, leaving trails of distorted air that made her eyes water and her vision blur. The space itself appeared wounded by the demon's passage, as if its presence was toxic to the natural order of things. The effect was disorientating, nauseating in a way that suggested her human senses weren't equipped to process what they were witnessing.

She rolled across the debris-strewn floor, coming up with her blade just as instinct screamed at her to move. The curved silver edge caught the dim light as she spun away from the demon's follow-up attack, ducking just in time as its backhand swept through the space where her head had been – delivered with enough force to decapitate. The concrete wall behind her exploded in a shower of dust and fragments, deep cracks radiating outward from the impact. Crumbling masonry filled the air, dust raining down like a grey snowfall, a stark reminder of the incredible power contained in the demon's deceptively human form. Had that blow connected with her skull, there wouldn't have been enough left to identify her dental records.

"Feisty," the demon purred, its voice carrying harmonics that no human throat could produce. It began circling her like a predator that had all the time in the world, its movements fluid and hypnotic despite the supernatural speed it had just displayed. "I do so enjoy a challenge. The easy ones break too quickly, provide such limited entertainment value. Though I suspect you'll break beautifully once I really begin to work on you."

There was something almost conversational about its tone, as if discussing torture and murder was no different from commenting on the weather. The casual nature of its threats was somehow more disturbing than screaming rage would have been – this was a creature that had turned suffering into a game, refined cruelty into a science.

Lianne kept moving, using what remained of the office furniture as cover while she assessed her opponent with the cold calculation that had kept her alive through countless battles with its kind. Broken chairs and overturned filing cabinets wouldn't provide much protection against something this powerful, but they might slow it down, force it to waste energy on obstacles while she looked for an opening.

This demon was significantly stronger than the simple possession cases she usually handled, the kind of minor entities that could be banished with the right ambush and a well-placed blade. Those were parasites, opportunistic feeders that latched onto human hosts like supernatural leeches. This thing was an apex predator. It had been feeding regularly for months, growing stronger with each kill. It was fast, and worst of all, intelligent enough to learn from its mistakes.

"You know," Lianne said, feinting left before slashing right with her blade in a move designed to test the demon's reflexes, "you talk too much for something that's about to die."

The demon's laughter thundered menacingly as it effortlessly avoided her strike – but her blade came closer than it expected. For a split second, surprise flickered across its adopted human features before the predatory smile returned.

"Such confidence," it said, lunging forward with inhuman speed. Its hand closed around her wrist in an iron grip that could have crushed bone, its smile widening to reveal teeth like black needles, each one sharp enough to punch through stone. "I wonder if you'll maintain that attitude when I start peeling your skin away in strips. I've found that even the bravest humans become remarkably co-operative once the real pain begins."

The pressure on her wrist was enormous,

threatening to snap the delicate bones like twigs. She could feel her circulation being cut off, her fingers beginning to tingle as the demon's grip tightened with inexorable force. In seconds, her hand would be useless, and then she'd be completely at this creature's mercy – and it was clear it had none to give.

Before it could follow through on the threat, something hit it from behind with the force of a freight train, the impact producing a sound like thunder in the confined space. The demon released Lianne instantly, spinning around with alarming speed to face its new attacker, its perfect composure finally showing cracks.

Mien stood in the doorway, no longer bothering to hide what she was behind human pretences. Her pale skin glowed with an eerie, otherworldly light that seemed to pulse from deep within. Her white-blonde hair whipped wildly around her face, as if caught in a fierce, unseen storm – defying gravity, twisting with currents that belonged to another realm entirely. The air around her crackled with unnatural energy, a clear warning that whatever she was now, it was far beyond anything human.

And when she opened her mouth, the sound that emerged was pure, concentrated death given voice.

The banshee's wail was unlike anything Lianne had ever heard, a sound that bypassed her ears and struck directly at the primitive parts of her brain responsible for recognising earthly danger. It was the cry of every mother who had lost a child, every lover who had watched their beloved die, every soul who had faced the end with nothing but regret for company. It was grief made tangible, sorrow given physical form and unleashed like a weapon.

The supernatural scream slammed into the demon, sending it staggering backward as though pushed by an invisible force. Windows didn't just break – they exploded outward in glittering cascades of glass that caught the city lights like fallen stars. Lianne, standing behind the banshee, had to clap her hands over her ears to block out the worst of it, her eardrums threatening to rupture from the sheer intensity of the sound. The wail seemed to go on forever, rising and falling in increasingly unbearable harmonics. This was what banshees were truly capable of when they abandoned all restraint.

And then, just as suddenly as it had begun, the scream cut off, leaving behind a ringing silence heavy with the echo of power. Lianne stood in awe, watching as Mien composed herself with ease – though her disgust for the creature before her was clear.

"Hello, Zuthan," Mien said, her voice now carrying an undertone of supernatural menace. The temperature in the room had dropped noticeably, frost beginning to form on the broken glass scattered across the floor. "Miss me?"

The use of a name transformed the encounter completely, turning what had been a straightforward hunt into something far more personal and dangerous. This wasn't just another demon feeding in the city's shadows – this was a creature with history, with connections to the banshee that went beyond simple predator and prey.

The demon's composure, already fraying, splintered further – its perfect businessman disguise buckling to reveal something raw and desperate beneath. "Mien," it said, and this time there was unmistakable emotion in its voice – recognition, and the brittle edge of fear. "I should have known you'd crawl out of whatever hole you've been hiding in. Still playing the grieving sister, I see."

"You killed my sister," Mien said, taking a few steps forward with deliberate, measured paces. Her supernatural glow intensified with each word, flooding the room with near-blinding flashes of light. "You made her watch while you tortured someone she loved. You fed on her horror, her helplessness, her love for him turning to despair. And when you were done with him, when there was nothing left of him to take, you started on her."

"She was delicious," Zuthan replied with a cruel smile that revealed more black needle teeth, his voice taking on a dreamy quality as if recalling a particularly fine meal. "Such exquisite despair, so perfectly seasoned with hope turned rancid. I savoured every moment of her suffering, let it marinate for hours before the final harvest. Though she did scream rather prettily at the end, I must admit."

The casual cruelty in his tone was designed to provoke, to turn Mien's grief into rage that could be exploited. Grief demons were masters of psychological warfare, understanding human emotions well enough to weaponise them against their owners. But banshees weren't human.

Mien's response was another wail, this one focused and targeted like a sonic lance designed to cut through steel. The sound hit Zuthan with surgical precision, and he threw himself aside with inhuman agility, barely avoiding the worst of the supernatural assault. Even the peripheral effects left him smoking and blistered, the perfect skin of his human disguise showing angry red welts where the banshee's power had touched him.

"Look at you, all desperate and hysterical," he said with a snarl, his humanlike shell beginning to crack and peel away like old paint. Something far worse was emerging from underneath, a twisted abomination of raw malice. "That's why you've failed to stop me before, and it's why you'll fail now. Sentiment makes you weak, predictable."

Lianne, momentarily forgotten in the middle of their supernatural standoff, took the opportunity to study both combatants with the wisdom of experience. The demon was incredibly powerful, its casual destruction of concrete walls and its relative nonchalance towards the banshee's initial attack implied a level of strength that could challenge small armies. But Mien's raw fury was something to behold, a force of nature given form and purpose that burned with the intensity of a collapsing star.

The problem was that fury could be a weakness as much as a strength, emotion clouding judgment and creating exploitable blind spots. Lianne had seen it happen before – hunters who let personal grudges override tactical thinking, usually right before something with claws separated their heads from their shoulders.

Zuthan seemed to realise this too, his survival instincts overriding whatever sadistic pleasure he took in taunting the vengeful banshee. His form began to shift and flow like something made of liquid shadow, the rest of the expensive suit melting away.

His skin darkened to a mottled grey-black, resembling ancient, rotting bark peeling away from a long-dead tree. His limbs stretched into spider-like appendages that twisted at impossible angles. His torso warped and contorted, taking on a grotesque form – utterly predatory and honed for lethal efficiency, crafted to evoke pure, primal terror.

But it was his face that completed the transformation from supposed-businessman to monster. What had been merely menacing became a shifting kaleidoscope of every person he'd ever killed, their features bleeding into one another in an endless parade of suffering. Eyes appeared and disappeared, mouths opened in silent screams before dissolving into new configurations of agony. It was as though he wore the faces of his victims like masks, each one a trophy from some past atrocity.

"Look closely, little banshee," he hissed, his voice now a chorus of the dead speaking in unison. "See all my beautiful children, my collection of exquisite moments. Your sister is in here somewhere, part of my eternal gallery. Would you like to hear her voice again?"

The psychological attack was precisely calculated, designed to exploit the one weakness all banshees shared – their connection to the dead, their inability to truly let go of those they'd failed to save. When the demon spoke again, Lianne noticed Mien's expression shift instantly, betraying the shock and pain that told her this was Elena's voice. She could only assume that it was perfectly reproduced – pleading and terrified in a way that cut through supernatural defences like a heated blade through butter.

"Mien, please, help me. It hurts so much. Why didn't you save me? I trusted you to protect me, and you let this happen. You let me die."

Lianne could see the words hitting Mien like physical blows, each accusation precisely aimed at the guilt that had been eating away at her for months. Her supernatural glow flickered like a candle in a high wind, and for a moment she looked deeply vulnerable, broken, haunted by failures both real and imagined.

"Elena?" she whispered, and there was such desperate hope in her voice that Lianne felt her heart clench in sympathy.

"That's not her," Lianne snapped, recognising the psychological warfare for what it was. She'd seen demons use similar tactics before. "It's a trick. Grief demons feed on guilt as much as suffering – don't give it what it wants."

But Mien wasn't listening. She was lost in a spiral of self-recrimination that had been months in the making. She was staring at Zuthan with something that might have been hope, and Lianne realised with growing alarm that the banshee was about to do something catastrophically stupid.

"Elena, I'm so sorry," Mien whispered, taking a step forward with her hands extended as if reaching for someone who might actually be there. "I should have protected you. I should have been there when you needed me. I should have…"

Zuthan struck while she was distracted, moving with the fluid speed of something that had perfected the art of killing over centuries of practice. His elongated limbs wrapped around her like steel cables, binding her arms to her sides and lifting her off the ground with contemptuous ease. Mien's glow began to dim, her strength draining away as the demon began to feed on her life force like an ethereal parasite.

"Mien!" Lianne moved without thinking, her blade carving through the air in a silver arc. Years of training and combat experience guided her strike, and the weapon bit deep into one of Zuthan's appendages, severing it completely in a spray of black ichor that hissed and steamed where it hit the floor.

The demon shrieked in raw agony, a savage howl that tore through the air. He released his grip on Mien, who collapsed to the floor, gasping and struggling to steady herself. Black blood splattered across the walls in sick, twisting patterns, and where it seeped into the concrete, the stone hissed and blistered as if corroded by some unholy venom.

"You stupid, sentimental imbecile," Zuthan growled, his borrowed voice cracking as pain shattered his concentration. The severed appendage writhed on the floor like a dying snake before dissolving into shadows that vanished with unnatural speed. "At least your sister knew what to do before the end. She stopped begging – eventually."

That was evidently the wrong thing to say. The mention of Elena's final moments became a catalyst, igniting Mien's grief into something far more dangerous. Her eyes blazed with renewed fury that seemed to burn away the last vestiges of restraint, her glow returning stronger than before. Power radiated from her in waves that made the air pulse violently with potential energy.

"You want to hear about the end?" she seethed, rising into the air like a vengeful storm about to be unleashed, lifted by volatile currents of raw, unyielding power. Her hair lashed around her face in chaotic spirals that tore through the space around her, and her eyes burned with a savage light – fierce and relentless. "Let me tell you about yours."

The wail that followed wasn't just sound – it was pure, distilled death given voice and purpose. The broken glass all around them didn't just shatter; it atomised, turning to glittering dust. The concrete walls cracked and splintered, fissures snaking like bloated, writhing worms burrowing frantically – relentless, invasive, and corrupting everything they touched. The metal framework of the building groaned in protest as forces beyond human understanding pressed against its structural integrity.

Zuthan, caught in the direct path of Mien's fury, began to unravel like flesh scorched by holy fire – shrivelling, splitting, collapsing under a power meant to purge abominations. His stolen faces wailed in unison as they sloughed off one by one, spectral masks disintegrating into ash and memory, each a monument to lives he'd devoured and defiled. His spider-like limbs buckled and tore, curling in on themselves before crumbling to soot.

Through it all, Mien's voice rose higher and higher, building to frequencies that seemed ready to tear holes in reality itself. The air began to vibrate in sympathy with her supernatural shriek, and Lianne could feel the sound resonating in her bones, in her teeth, in the deepest parts of her soul where primal fears lived and multiplied.

Lianne edged back as far as the crumbling space would allow, instinctively seeking distance from the raw force before her. She watched in a mixture of fascination and terror. This was what banshees were capable of when they stopped holding back – when they shed every last vestige of subtlety and restraint and became their full, terrifying selves.

In a state of sheer panic, Zuthan made a desperate attempt to escape, his dissolving form lunging towards a broken window in a bid for freedom, driven by survival instincts refined over eons. For a moment, it looked like he might make it, but Mien was ready for him. Her wail shifted, becoming a net of pure sound that caught him in a firm grip, holding him suspended in the air like an insect trapped in amber. The acoustic web tightened around him, each strand composed of frequencies that existed on the boundary between sound and death, between noise and oblivion.

Zuthan screamed – a hellish sound with no trace of defiance, but soul-deep terror. The sound clashed violently with Mien's shriek, a disharmony so intense it was almost unbearable. The demon's form began to buckle under the pressure. Shadow peeled away from him like burning skin, revealing not flesh, but the writhing, howling essence of something that had never been human and had no right to exist in any world governed by natural laws.

The last of the stolen faces twisted and shrieked as they were flayed from him one by one, spinning into the air before disintegrating into motes of black ash. His scream faltered, broke, and then finally died as the last shreds of his being unravelled into nothingness.

With a final, deafening crescendo, Mien's wail reached its peak – and then abruptly stopped.

The silence that followed was cataclysmic. It wasn't the gentle absence of sound, but a vacuum, a pressure drop that made Lianne's ears ring and her knees threaten to buckle. Zuthan was simply... gone. Not dead in the traditional sense, but eradicated – every trace of him scrubbed from the fabric of the world like a stain too foul to be allowed to linger.

Dust swirled through the ruined space in slow, spiralling drifts. The floor was cratered where he'd hung suspended – scorched and cracked like something ancient and blighted. Lianne, braced against what was left of a support beam, stared at the void left behind, her breath catching in her throat. There was no body. No remains. Only the distant echo of a power that had tried to defy death – and failed.

Mien hovered in the air for a breathless moment, her glow dimming, her shoulders sagging. Then, like a marionette whose strings had been cut, she dropped lightly to the ground, her feet touching down with a whisper.

Lianne didn't speak. She wouldn't have been able to find the words even if she'd wanted to. She simply watched as the banshee stood amidst the wreckage she had wrought, haloed in silence.

"For Elena," Mien said simply.

Chapter Five

The silence that followed Zuthan's destruction was almost as unsettling as the chaos that had preceded it, a heavy quiet that seemed to press against Lianne's ears like cotton. The air itself felt different now, lighter somehow, as if a great weight had been lifted from the world. Beyond the broken windows, somewhere in the distance, the city continued its eternal hum, oblivious to the supernatural battle that had just concluded.

Mien stood motionless amidst the wreckage, the supernatural glow around her fading gradually until she looked almost like her old self. Almost, except for the way her eyes still held flecks of starlight that seemed to shift and swirl in patterns that hurt to look at directly, and the faint aura of otherworldly power that clung to her like strong perfume. Even diminished, her presence filled the room with potential energy, the sense that she could unleash a devastating torrent of force again at a moment's notice.

The transformation was subtle but profound – her hair settled into more natural patterns, no longer defying gravity with paranormal currents, and her skin lost its inner illumination, becoming merely pale rather than luminescent. But there was something in her posture, in the way she held herself, that revealed the aftermath of violence and the grim satisfaction of long-delayed justice.

"Is it over?" The male victim's voice was barely a whisper, no doubt hoarse from screaming and dehydration, but in the sudden quiet it seemed to carry through the space with startling clarity. His eyes darted between Lianne, Mien, and the empty space where Zuthan had been destroyed, as if he couldn't quite believe that his tormentor was truly gone.

Lianne crouched beside him, her professional instinct overriding the adrenaline that still coursed through her veins. She checked his pulse; it was elevated but steady. He was alive, and that was more than many of Zuthan's victims could claim.

"Yeah, it's over," she said, keeping her voice gentle and reassuring despite the violence that continued replaying in her mind. "We need to get you both to a hospital."

"No hospitals," Mien said quietly, her voice carrying an undertone of authority that brooked no argument. She stared at the empty space where the demon had been – an absence that spoke louder than any body could. Her expression was hard to read – satisfaction tangled with a trace of something colder, maybe disappointment, as if the revenge she'd sought for so long had proven less fulfilling than she imagined. "Too many questions. Paperwork. Investigations that dig into things better left buried. I know someone who can help them, no questions asked."

The practical considerations of their situation were already asserting themselves. Hospital staff would want to know how the victims had sustained their injuries, where they'd been held, who was responsible for their condition. Police would be called, reports would be filed, and eventually someone would start asking the kind of questions that could expose the supernatural community to scrutiny it couldn't afford.

Lianne's phone buzzed with an incoming call, the vibration startling in the tense moment. She glanced suspiciously at the screen – it was her client from the other night.

"Cross," she answered, stepping away from the victims to avoid distressing them further with whatever crisis was about to unfold.

"Ms Cross, thank God." The man's voice was tight with panic. There was genuine terror there. "There's been... there's another one. In my building. Floor seven. Please, you have to come back. I'll pay anything, anything at all."

Lianne felt a cold knot forming in her stomach, the kind of dread that came from recognising patterns that pointed to trouble. "Another one?"

"Yeah, but it's... It's..." His voice cracked, the careful control of a successful businessman completely giving way to naked fear. "It's asking for you by name. It knows who you are, what you do. It's been waiting for you."

The implications hit her hard. If demons were starting to learn her name, to target her specifically, then the careful balance she'd maintained for the entirety of her hunting career was beginning to collapse.

She ended the call and turned to find Mien watching her with knowing eyes that seemed to see more than they should. The banshee's expression was thoughtful, calculating, as if she was already working through the tactical ramifications of whatever she'd overheard.

"Problem?" the banshee asked, though her tone suggested she already knew the answer.

"Maybe," Lianne answered, aware of the nervousness in her voice. She ran a hand through her hair. The strands were gritty with concrete dust and other debris, a tactile reminder of how quickly violence could erupt in her line of work. "The demon I killed for my last client – it might have had friends."

"Bastard." Mien was already moving towards the victims, her manner becoming endearingly gentle as she shifted from supernatural anomaly to caregiver with the fluid ease of someone accustomed to multiple roles.

Lianne watched with growing respect as Mien gently helped the man to his feet, speaking to him in a voice so soft and comforting that it was hard to believe the same woman had just unleashed enough destructive power to destroy a building. The contrast was jarring – one moment a figure of blistering paranormal fury, the next an empath tending to trauma victims with infinite patience.

There were depths to this banshee that Lianne was only beginning to understand, layers of personality and experience that suggested a history far more complex than their brief partnership had revealed. The way she handled the victims spoke to medical training or at least extensive experience with trauma care, while her earlier tactical planning had demonstrated strategic thinking that went far beyond simple vengeance.

"I need to go," Lianne said, checking her equipment automatically. "If there's a demon targeting me specifically, I can't ignore it.

Letting threats fester only makes them more dangerous."

"Then I'm coming with you." Mien had both victims on their feet now, supporting them with surprising gentleness for someone who had just torn apart a demon with nothing but her voice. The elderly woman leaned heavily against her, still desperately weak from prolonged captivity, while the man clutched her arm with the urgent grip of someone desperate to leave all physical reminders of his torture behind. "Just give me twenty minutes to get these two to someone who can help."

"This isn't your fight," Lianne said, though even as the words left her mouth she knew they were probably futile. The banshee had already demonstrated a disturbing tendency to insert herself into dangerous situations, and the partnership that had begun as a matter of mutual convenience was starting to feel like something more permanent.

"After what just happened here, I'll be damned if I'm going to let another demon walk free." Mien paused, studying Lianne's face with those storm-coloured eyes. "Besides, you might need backup. And I owe you one for earlier."

The admission of debt was significant, Lianne realised. Mien seemed to take such obligations seriously, perhaps bound by codes of honour older than human civilisation. Whatever had been building between them during their brief partnership, Mien now considered herself obliged to provide assistance – a development that could prove either invaluable or catastrophic.

Lianne wanted to argue, to maintain the professional distance that had kept her alive through a decade of solo hunting, but the practical side of her mind recognised the truth in Mien's words. If demons were specifically targeting her, if her anonymity had been compromised, then having a banshee ally wasn't the worst idea she'd ever had.

"Twenty minutes," she agreed, checking the time on her phone. "Meet me at Aguar Tower. Seventh floor."

Mien nodded, already guiding the victims towards the exit. "Be careful, Lianne. If this thing knows your name, it's been watching you for a while. That means it knows your methods, your weapons, and probably your weaknesses too."

Chapter Six

Lianne moved cautiously through the maze of back alleys, keeping to the shadows to avoid drawing attention. The city was still cloaked in the pre-dawn hush, its streets almost deserted except for the occasional distant rumble of a delivery truck or a solitary dog barking in the distance. Pools of orange and white light bathed the cracked pavement beneath her boots. With every step, her mind churned, and the more she thought, the less she liked the conclusions she was reaching.

Demons didn't usually operate in co-ordinated groups, their territorial nature and competitive instincts making long-term alliances difficult to maintain. But they weren't above using each other when it served their purposes, forming temporary partnerships based on mutual benefit rather than genuine co-operation. Indeed, if Zuthan had been working with others, sharing information or resources, then his death might have triggered some kind of retaliation. The thought made Lianne's shoulders tense and her pace quicken, her boots striking the pavement with renewed urgency.

Aguar Tower rose from the heart of the city like a monument to urban luxury, its towering glass shimmering with reflected city lights. At this hour, the grounds should have been nearly silent. Instead, Lianne spotted police cars, their red and blue lights painting the surrounding buildings in alternating waves of colour. Several ambulances lined the street, and she could see paramedics wheeling a gurney out of the building's main entrance, carrying a sheet-covered form that told its own grim story. The scene had the kind of multi-agency response that usually followed mass casualties. Yellow tape cordoned off a two-block radius.

Lianne approached one of the officers stationed behind the yellow tape, her boots crunching softly against the asphalt. The young man straightened as she drew near, hand drifting instinctively towards his belt – until she met his eyes.

"I'm a hunter," she said, her voice calm, professional.

Recognition flickered across his face. No questions, no badge check. Just a sharp nod and a silent step aside. They both understood. Whatever was waiting inside, this wasn't something the police could handle.

The lift ride to the seventh floor gave Lianne time to prepare mentally for whatever she was about to encounter. The interior was all marble and mahogany, the kind of understated luxury that suggested serious money and influence – but as the soft chime announced her arrival and the doors slid open, the illusion shattered.

Lianne stepped into chaos. The entire floor, once a collection of luxury apartments furnished with the kind of curated excess only the truly wealthy could afford, now looked like a war zone. Furniture lay overturned and shattered, priceless décor reduced to rubble. The air reeked of sulphur and something worse. The coppery tang of blood mixed with ozone and scorched materials, a scent that spoke of violence both mundane and otherworldly.

"Ms Cross?" Detective Ray Morrison stepped out of one of the apartments, his face pale and drawn, making him look older than his forty-something years. Lianne had helped him before – cases that officially didn't exist, the ones buried under red tape or blamed on gas leaks and electrical fires. "Thank Christ you're here. This thing... it's not like the others."

Morrison was one of the few in law enforcement who understood the city's supernatural undercurrent – a detective who'd seen enough impossible things to accept that the world was stranger and more dangerous than most realised. His presence here meant whatever had happened was serious enough to call in specialists, bad enough that normal procedures had been tossed aside for damage control.

"Show me," she said, following him down the hallway.

"Three dead so far, all residents," Morrison said, his voice taking on a clipped professional tone of detachment. "The thing killed them fast, efficiently. No torture, no games. Just... execution. Clean, precise, almost surgical in its approach."

They stopped outside an apartment doorway. The remains of the door hung crooked, splintered by whatever force had struck it. Morrison handed her a piece of paper. "It left this."

The note was written on expensive stationery paper, in what looked like blood. The handwriting was elegant, flowing script that felt eerily out of place:

Ms Cross,

You facilitated the killing of my associate tonight. I propose a trade: your life for the lives of all the residents of this building. I've already killed a few as a warning. I can come back for the others. I advise you to work with me on this.

– D.

"D?" Lianne muttered, studying the handwriting for clues about its author, but finding nothing.

"Whatever it is, it's smart," Morrison said. "It's as though this thing had it all planned out like a military strike – we found the security system completely disabled when we arrived."

The tactical sophistication was disturbing, suggesting an opponent who understood human technology and psychology well enough to exploit both. Most demons were creatures of instinct and tradition, relying on supernatural power rather than careful planning. This one had approached the situation with the methodical precision of a professional, which made it exponentially more dangerous.

Lianne's mind churned through possibilities, piecing together what little she knew, trying to get ahead of something already several steps beyond her.

"Well now," the lilting voice of an unfamiliar female drawled behind them, smooth as silk and laced with mockery. "Surprise really is the soul of theatre, wouldn't you agree?"

They turned to see a woman standing at the end of the hallway, perfectly positioned for maximum dramatic impact. She was incredibly beautiful – perfect features, perhaps enhanced by something supernatural: flawless skin that seemed to glow with inner health, and a poise so natural it suggested power and influence beneath the surface.

Her long black dress was haute couture, cut to emphasise her figure while maintaining an air of sophisticated elegance. Her hair was styled in a classic up-do that showcased the graceful line of her neck, and her jewellery was understated yet unmistakably precious – the kind of pieces passed down through generations of wealth.

Only her eyes gave her away, burning with an inner fire that had nothing to do with humanity and everything to do with powers beyond human comprehension.

Morrison's hand moved instinctively towards his weapon.

The demon smiled with genuine amusement. "Don't worry, dear. There's nothing here for you to worry about." Her gaze shifted to Lianne with predatory interest. "But you... you must be the famous demon hunter. I must say, your reputation precedes you."

"You're D," Lianne said, her hand finding the grip of her blade.

"Duchess Dantalion, at your service." The demon executed a perfect curtsy, the gesture somehow managing to be both mocking and elegant, as if she were simultaneously paying respect and making fun of the entire concept of human courtesy. "I believe you facilitated the killing of an associate of mine earlier this evening. Zuthan was crude, admittedly, lacking in social graces and aesthetic sensibility, but he served his purpose. His death, however, has created certain... complications."

"Such as?"

"Balance, Ms Cross. Equilibrium. The supernatural community in this city operates on a delicate ecosystem, carefully maintained through centuries of negotiation and occasional violence." Dantalion began walking towards them, her heels clicking on the marble floor with the precise rhythm of a metronome. "Demons, spirits, the occasional vampire – we all have our territories, our feeding grounds, our mutual agreements that prevent open warfare in the streets. Zuthan may have been a brute, but he kept the lower-tier demons in line, maintained order through fear and occasional demonstration of superior power."

Lianne felt the pieces clicking into place in her mind, the tactical situation resolving into something that made sense from a supernatural politics perspective. "So you want to take his place."

"I want to maintain order, prevent chaos, ensure the delicate balance we've established doesn't collapse into open warfare that would expose us all to human scrutiny." Dantalion stopped just out of arm's reach, her perfect smile never faltering despite the serious nature of their conversation. "But certain parties in our community feel that anyone who works with others – as you do – can't be trusted to maintain the status quo. Hence our current situation. I simply need to kill you, prove my commitment to the old ways, and assume Zuthan's territory. That way, everyone wins."

"Except me."

"Well, yes," Dantalion said with a small shrug that somehow made murder seem like a minor inconvenience. "Except you."

Before Lianne could draw her weapon or Morrison could scramble for cover, everything turned to black with the finality of a closing coffin lid.

Chapter Seven

The darkness was absolute, pressing against Lianne's eyes like velvet suffocation. It wasn't merely the absence of light – it was darkness given weight and substance, a living thing that seemed to crawl across exposed skin with fingers made of shadow and malice. The emergency lighting that should have kicked in remained dormant, the backup systems apparently as compromised as everything else in the building.

Lianne pressed her back against the wall, feeling the cool marble as every sense strained to locate Dantalion in the sudden void. The texture of the stone was reassuring, a solid anchor in a world that had suddenly become fluid and dangerous. Her breathing seemed unnaturally loud in the oppressive quiet, and she fought to control it, knowing that any sound could betray her position to something that hunted with senses far keener than human perception.

Somewhere in the distance, she could hear Detective Morrison calling her name, his voice tight with panic and confusion, but the sound seemed to come from miles away rather than the few dozen feet that actually separated them. The acoustics of the hallway had been warped by whatever supernatural force Dantalion was wielding, turning the space into a freakish landscape where normal rules no longer applied.

"Afraid of the dark, Ms Cross?" Dantalion's voice drifted from everywhere and nowhere all at once, echoing off surfaces that shouldn't exist in the confined space of a residential hallway. The words seemed to come from the walls themselves, from the ceiling, from the very air around her. "Most humans are. It's such a primal fear, isn't it? The unknown lurking just beyond sight, the certainty that something with teeth and claws is watching from the shadows."

The demon's voice carried traces of amusement, as if this deadly game of supernatural hide-and-seek was nothing more than an entertaining diversion. There was something almost intimate about her tone, the way she spoke as if they were old friends sharing secrets rather than predator and prey circling each other in the dark.

A whisper of displaced air made Lianne duck instinctively, her combat reflexes overriding conscious thought. Razor-sharp claws raked the wall where her head had been, gouging deep furrows in the marble that would have split her skull like brittle bone. Stone dust rained down on her shoulders, and she could smell the sulphur scent that clung to the demon's form.

She rolled sideways, came up with her blade ready, but struck only empty space when she lashed out at where she thought Dantalion might be. The silver edge whistled through the darkness, meeting no resistance, and Lianne had to bite back a curse at the wasted motion. Dantalion was toying with her, wielding the darkness like a weapon, forcing her to fight blind.

"You know what I find fascinating about your kind?" the demon said conversationally, her voice shifting position as she spoke, circling like a shark in black water. "You hunt monsters that could tear you apart without breaking a sweat, all for money. What drives someone to choose such a life? What childhood trauma or psychological deficiency pushes a person towards a profession with such appalling mortality rates?"

The questions were designed to distract, to make her think about anything other than the immediate tactical situation. Demons were masters of psychological warfare, understanding that doubt and hesitation could be more effective than claws and fangs when it came to disarming human opponents.

Lianne didn't answer, focusing instead on the subtle sounds that could give away the demon's position: the whisper of fabric against skin as Dantalion moved through the darkness, the distinctive click of designer heels on marble, the faint sulphur scent that seemed to be coming from...

She spun and slashed, her blade carving through the air in a perfect arc. This time she connected, feeling the weapon bite deep into something that wasn't quite flesh but wasn't quite spirit either. The demon screamed in a voice like metal torn and twisted under unbearable strain, a sound that seemed to bypass Lianne's ears and strike directly at the primitive parts of her brain responsible for recognising mortal danger.

The lights came back on all at once, harsh fluorescents blazing to life with the suddenness of a camera flash. The abrupt transition from absolute darkness to brilliant illumination left Lianne blinking and disorientated, struggling to adjust to the sudden sensory overload.

Dantalion stood pressed against the opposite wall, one perfectly manicured hand clamped over a deep gash in her shoulder. Black ichor seeped between her fingers, hissing and steaming where it hit the polished floor like drops of liquid acid. Her perfect composure had cracked, revealing something wild and dangerous beneath the cultured façade.

"First blood to you," the demon said, though her perfect smile never wavered despite the obvious pain she was experiencing. There was genuine surprise in her voice, as if she hadn't expected a mere mortal to land such a clean hit. "I'm impressed. Most humans would still be cowering in the corner, paralysed by terror and the sudden absence of their primary sense."

"Most humans don't make a living killing things like you," Lianne replied, keeping her blade ready while she assessed the tactical situation. The wound was deep but not immediately fatal, and she could already see the edges beginning to knit together.

Dantalion pushed herself away from the wall, her wound now beginning to close with the kind of accelerated healing that made some supernatural beings so difficult to kill. The black ichor continued to hiss where it touched the floor, eating through the expensive marble like industrial solvent.

"True enough," she said, straightening her dress with an almost automatic elegance. "Though I wonder... have you ever considered that perhaps we're not so different, you and I? We both kill for practical reasons rather than passion. We both survive by being better predators than our prey, more cunning than our opponents, willing to do whatever it takes to emerge victorious."

The comparison was designed to unsettle, to plant seeds of doubt about the righteousness of her cause. It was a classic demon tactic – make the hunter question their own motivations, blur the line between good and evil until moral certainty became moral ambiguity.

"I don't torture innocent people for fun," Lianne said, though even as the words left her mouth she could hear the defensive edge in her voice.

"Don't you?" Dantalion tilted her head, studying Lianne with genuine curiosity that seemed oddly out of place given their circumstances. "Tell me, how many demons have you killed in your career? How many supernatural beings have you hunted and slaughtered for money, without ever bothering to learn their names or understand their stories? Do you ever wonder if some of them might have been trying to change, to be better than their nature dictated?"

The question hit closer to home than Lianne wanted to admit, striking at doubts she'd buried beneath years of professional necessity and moral simplification. In ten years of hunting, she'd never bothered to ask if any of her targets had families, hopes, dreams beyond their paranormal hunger. They were monsters, and monsters existed to be killed. It was a simple equation that had never required deeper examination, a moral framework that made the violence necessary and the guilt manageable.

"Doubt is such a useful weapon," Dantalion continued, apparently reading Lianne's thoughts with an insight that came from centuries of manipulating human psychology. "It's killed more heroes than all the demons in hell combined. The moment you start questioning whether your cause is just, whether your methods are moral, you've already lost half the battle."

Before Lianne could respond, before she could formulate a defence against the psychological assault, the temperature in the hallway dropped to a biting cold. Her breath became visible in the suddenly frigid air, and frost began forming on the walls like delicate glass flowers blooming in fast-forward. The air itself seemed to crystallise around them, heavy with the unmistakable imprint of supernatural forces bending reality to their will.

"Sorry I'm late," Mien's voice cut through the cold like a heated blade through ice, carrying undertones of power that made the very atmosphere tremble.

The banshee materialised out of the shadows at the far end of the hallway, her pale form seeming to step out of darkness itself, as if shadow was simply another doorway she could use at will. Her glow cast everything in stark relief, creating dramatic contrasts of light and shadow that transformed the hallway into something from a classical painting of divine judgment.

But something was different about her now, something that made Lianne's professional instincts sit up and take notice. The light she radiated wasn't just ethereal – it was aggressive, predatory, like moonlight reflected off a naked blade. There was violence in her luminescence, a promise of death that suggested power barely held in check.

Dantalion's composure didn't just crack – it splintered, her perfect mask of sophisticated elegance slipping to reveal something that might have been genuine dread. "A banshee," she said, smoothing her dress with a hand that didn't quite hide its tremble. "How delightfully unexpected."

"Another demon," Mien replied, mockingly blunt. "How disappointingly predictable. The city's practically overrun with your kind these days." Her storm-coloured gaze flicked to Lianne. "You ok?"

"Peachy. Just having a philosophical discussion about the nature of good and evil," Lianne said, grateful for the backup despite her professional preference for working alone.

"Sounds boring," Mien said with a grin that was sharp enough to cut diamonds and twice as brilliant. "How about we skip to the part where we kill the demon and get out of here?"

Dantalion laughed, the sound echoing off the walls, each note carrying traces of power that made the air vibrate in sympathy. "Two overconfident little optimists thinking numbers can overcome power? I almost feel sorry for you both. Almost. Though I suppose you've managed to make things marginally more interesting."

She moved then, her form becoming a blur of motion that defied the laws of physics. But instead of attacking Lianne, she went for Mien, perhaps recognising the banshee as the greater threat or simply preferring to eliminate the supernatural opponent first. Her claws extended into razor-sharp talons that gleamed like polished obsidian as she closed the distance in a flash of unearthly speed.

Mien didn't dodge, didn't attempt to evade the attack through superior agility or tactical positioning. Instead, she opened her mouth and let loose with a wail that turned the air solid, transforming the atmosphere into a weapon. The sound hit Dantalion like a physical wall, stopping her charge cold and sending her skidding backward across the polished floor with her hands pressed to her ears in a futile attempt to block out the intolerable assault.

"My turn," Lianne said.

She attacked while the demon was still stunned and disorientated. Her blade found its mark, sinking deep into Dantalion's side, the silver edge parting unnatural flesh like butter. The demon shrieked in pain and surprise, her perfect features contorting into something far less human, far more honest about her true nature.

Black veins began spreading across her skin like a web of infection, and her eyes blazed with sheer fury. The elegant disguise was finally falling away, revealing the monster that had always lurked beneath the surface of sophistication and culture.

"Enough games," Dantalion snarled, her neatly-accented voice becoming something guttural and strange, as if her vocal cords were no longer adequate to express the rage burning within her supernatural form. "If you both want to die so badly, I'll gladly accommodate. Consider it a professional courtesy."

The hallway exploded into chaos as Dantalion abandoned all pretence of humanity. She became a whirlwind of claws and fangs, her human disguise falling away completely to reveal something monstrous, the pure embodiment of nightmares, raw and terrifying.

Her form stretched and twisted, her limbs elongating beyond human proportions while her fingers became talons sharp enough to part steel. Her face lost all semblance of human beauty, becoming something that hurt to look at directly, a shifting kaleidoscope of predatory features that seemed designed to instil maximum terror in potential prey.

She struck at both women simultaneously, her movements too fast to follow with normal human perception, forcing them apart and onto the defensive. The confined space of the hallway became a three-dimensional battlefield where every surface could be used for attack or evasion.

Lianne found herself pressed back against the wall, barely managing to deflect the demon's attacks with her blade. Each impact sent shockwaves up her arms, the force of the blows threatening to numb her hands and make her weapon useless. She could feel her strength beginning to fade, her human limitations asserting themselves against an opponent whose power seemed limitless.

This demon was far beyond the simple possession cases she usually handled, creatures that could be banished with the right strategy and a well-placed blade. This was something that could challenge small armies, a force of supernatural destruction that had been refined over centuries of existence into an engine of perfect lethality.

Mien was faring better, her supernatural nature allowing her to match Dantalion's speed and ferocity, but even she was being driven back step by step. The banshee's wails had become a constant thing, turning the air around them into a weapon that struck from all directions, but Dantalion seemed to be adapting to the assault with the kind of tactical intelligence that made her exponentially more dangerous.

"You can't win," the demon taunted, landing a glancing blow that sent Lianne spinning into the wall hard enough to crack the marble. "I've been killing for centuries, perfecting the art of murder through sheer repetition and natural talent. You're children playing with forces you don't understand, amateurs trying to challenge a master of the craft."

That's when Lianne realised something

crucial – a tactical insight born of desperation and hard-earned experience. Dantalion was right: in a straight fight, they couldn't win. The demon was too strong, too fast, too skilled in the art of violence. But this wasn't a straight fight. It was an ambush in a confined space. The demon might be stronger, but she was also trapped by the environment in ways Lianne and Mien weren't.

"Mien!" she called out, dodging another swipe of razor-sharp claws that left deep gouges in the wall where her head had been. "The sprinkler system!"

The banshee's eyes lit up with understanding. "On it!"

Instead of directing her wail at Dantalion, Mien turned her attention to the ceiling, her voice rising to frequencies that existed on the boundary between sound and pure destructive force. The acoustic assault hit the fire suppression system like a sledgehammer, shattering pipes and sending water cascading down in torrents that transformed the previously elegant hallway into an impromptu waterfall.

Within seconds, the entire seventh floor was flooded ankle-deep, carpets and designer furnishings soaking up the deluge like expensive sponges. The ice-cold water, likely drawn from the building's rooftop storage tanks, spread across the marble floor in patterns that caught the light like scattered diamonds.

"Water?" Dantalion said, confused and not bothering to conceal her amusement. "What's next? Going to throw soap at me? Perhaps some nice bath salts to make this more relaxing?"

Lianne smiled grimly and pulled a small vial from her equipment belt, the glass container no larger than her thumb but containing something far more potent than its size suggested. "Not soap. Holy water – just a tiny amount of this will sanctify every last drop around us."

She'd heard about the trick from someone who knew a priest who'd once had to deal with a vampire infestation in his church basement. The problem had required creative solutions and a willingness to think outside conventional parameters. Holy water didn't lose its sacred properties when diluted

– it just spread them around, turning ordinary water into a weapon that could deeply impact supernatural beings.

Lianne kept her gaze locked on Dantalion as she removed the stopper from the vial with a deliberate twist. The faint scent of myrrh and ozone drifted up as she tilted the glass, releasing a single, glimmering drop towards the ankle-deep water pooling around her boots.

It struck the surface with barely a ripple, but that subtle tremor unfurled and began to spread, gathering force as it went. A shimmer pulsed outward like lightning beneath glass, racing across the floor in every direction. The water caught the light unnaturally, glowing faintly, as if stirred to life by some invisible current. The sanctified essence rippled through the flooded space like a living thing. The air seemed to tighten, charged with divine intent. Dantalion froze, her expression shifting from disdain to horrified recognition. For the first time, the balance of power was tipping, and Lianne didn't look away for a second.

Dantalion's features twisted from horrified recognition into something closer to panic as the sanctified water began to eat through her like industrial acid. Steam rose from her body in writhing columns of vapour, the scent of burning corruption thick in the air. Her body contorted in raw, unfiltered agony, and her inhuman shriek tore through the hallway with such force that the walls trembled, the floor and its ankle-deep water shuddering like the beginnings of an earthquake.

"You clever little..." The demon's words were cut off as Mien's next wail struck her full in the chest, the acoustic assault sending her sliding backward through the blessed water. Wherever the liquid touched, the demon's form began to dissolve, supernatural flesh unable to maintain coherence in the embrace of sanctified fluid.

But even wounded and burning, with her very essence consumed by holy water, the demon showed no sign of surrender. Her movements grew more desperate, sharper – an instinct honed over centuries of survival. It was clear she understood the danger of complacency – that vital moment when an opponent believed they'd won.

With a roar of anguish that shook the

building's framework, the demon lunged at Lianne in one final, desperate attack – claws extended, death written in her blazing eyes, her dissolving form gathering every remaining ounce of power for a last strike aimed at Lianne's throat.

Lianne met her halfway, her blade punching through the demon's chest in a perfect thrust that struck the core of the creature's essence with surgical precision. Time seemed to shatter around them – predator and prey locked in a brutal standoff, two forces suspended on the razor's edge between life and oblivion, their final dance a deadly testament to will and fury.

"Well played," the demon whispered, black ichor frothing from her lips like dark champagne. Her voice carried traces of genuine respect, as if she were acknowledging a worthy opponent even in the moment of her destruction. "Perhaps... perhaps there is something to be said for... human determination after all."

Then she crumbled to ash, her perfect form dissolving like sand in the wind. The fine ash drifted down, settling into the ankle-deep water, where it swirled and slowly dispersed, vanishing as if swallowed by a sanctified flood.

The sudden absence of the demon's presence felt like a weight lifted from the world, the oppressive atmosphere she'd created dissipating like smoke. The silence was broken only by the steady drip of water from the ruined sprinkler system, a rhythmic percussion that seemed almost musical after the chaos of furious combat. Lianne surveyed the wreckage with the kind of professional interest that came from years of cleaning up after supernatural incidents, while Mien leaned against the wall, exhausted both physically and emotionally.

"That was tougher than I expected," the banshee said, wringing water from her white-blonde hair with movements that somehow managed to be elegant despite their practical nature.

"Most hunts are," Lianne replied, checking her equipment with automatic efficiency and mentally cataloguing what needed to be addressed. Her blade would require cleaning, and her holy water supply would have to be replenished before the next job. "Thanks for the backup. It made all the difference."

"Perhaps," Mien said, a modest smile tugging at the corner of her lips, revealing a flash of her needle-sharp teeth. "You handled yourself well though. Besides, you've been working alone for all these years. That holy water trick was inspired."

Detective Morrison appeared at the end of the hallway, his heavy boots splashing through the water as he took in the destruction with the weary resignation of someone who'd seen too much over the years and had long since given up trying to make sense of it all. Water damage, shattered windows, and the lingering scent of sulphur and ozone.

"Please tell me it's over," he said, his voice heavy with exhaustion after a night marked by death and chaos.

"It's over," Lianne confirmed. "The demon is dead. The building's safe."

"Good. Because I'm getting too old for this." Morrison pulled out his radio, already preparing to co-ordinate the kind of operation that would bury the entire incident beneath layers of bureaucratic red tape and insurance claims. "I'll need a clean-up crew in here, and someone's going to have to explain the water damage to the building's management."

As the detective liaised with his team, Mien moved closer to Lianne, her presence a cold comfort in the aftermath of violence. "Come on," she said. "Let's get out of here."

Chapter Eight

A mile from Aguar Tower, the industrial chaos of their supernatural battle felt like a half-remembered nightmare, softened by distance and the growing light of dawn. Lianne and Mien had kept to the shadows, threading through back alleys and forgotten spaces where the city's underbelly breathed in the quiet hours before the morning rush. Lianne's boots echoed softly on wet pavement still slick from the night's earlier rain, and the air carried the familiar urban cocktail of exhaust fumes, coffee from early-opening cafés, and the lingering ozone scent that always followed paranormal violence.

They stopped in a narrow alleyway between two ageing brick buildings. Lianne leaned on a wall, aware of its rough texture as her body finally began to process the night's accumulated adrenaline. Every muscle ached with the kind of exhaustion that came from sustained combat, and she could feel minor cuts and bruises making themselves known now that the immediate danger had passed.

Mien stood a few feet away, her glow dimmed to barely perceptible levels, making her look almost human in the growing dawn light. Almost, except for the way the early morning shadows seemed to bend around her slightly. Her ethereal beauty was somehow more pronounced in the quiet aftermath of violence.

"Well," the banshee said finally, breaking the comfortable silence that had settled between them, her voice carrying traces of exhaustion. "That was certainly a night I won't forget anytime soon."

"Tell me about it," Lianne replied, running a hand through her hair and feeling the grit of concrete dust and other debris from their recent encounters. "Though I have to say, it's not every night I get to team up with a banshee to take down two demons, one after the other. That's got to be some kind of record."

Mien's laugh was soft, carrying none of the supernatural harmonics that had made her wails so deadly. It was filled with genuine warmth and the kind of camaraderie that came from shared danger and mutual respect. "I can't thank you enough for what you did tonight, Lianne. Because of you, I finally got the chance to face Zuthan. It means more than I can properly express."

The sincerity in her voice was unmistakable, cutting through any pretence or supernatural mystique to reveal something raw and honest beneath. Lianne found herself oddly moved by the admission, recognising the extent of grief that had been driving the banshee's actions for months.

"It won't bring Elena back," Mien continued, her storm-coloured eyes distant as she stared up at the lightening sky visible between the buildings. "Nothing can do that. But at least now I can grieve properly, without the constant ache of knowing her killer is still out there, still hurting others, still profiting from her suffering. There's a kind of peace in that, I suppose. Closure, even if it's not the kind anyone would choose."

Lianne nodded, understanding the sentiment better than she might have expected. In her decade of hunting, she'd met plenty of people seeking vengeance for supernatural crimes, and most of them discovered revenge was rarely as satisfying as anticipated. The dead remained dead, the past unchanged, but sometimes the living could find a way to move forward.

"For what it's worth," she said, "I feel your sister would have been proud of you tonight. The way you fought for her, the way you never gave up – that takes real strength."

Mien's smile was bittersweet, touched with sadness but also genuine gratitude. "Thank you. That... that actually means more than you know." She paused, seeming to gather herself before continuing. "I think I'm done with demon hunting though. This was personal, a debt that needed settling, but I don't plan on making a habit of it. I'm not cut out for this kind of life – too much emotion, not enough detachment. Tonight proved that."

"It's probably for the best," Lianne agreed, though she found herself oddly disappointed by the admission. Working with Mien had been surprisingly effective, their different skills complementing each other in ways that made them exponentially more dangerous as a team. "I'm happy to go back to working solo anyway. Partnerships can draw the wrong kind of attention – Dantalion proved that. When demons start seeing hunters as a co-ordinated threat rather than individual operators, things can get messy – and fast!"

"Exactly," Mien said, clearly relieved that Lianne understood without taking offence. "You've been doing this for years on your own, building a reputation, establishing your territory. The last thing you need is some emotional banshee dragging you into supernatural politics and ancient grudges."

They stood quietly for a moment, both processing the events of the night and the inevitable end of their brief partnership. The city continued to wake around them – more traffic in the distance, the rumble of delivery trucks making their early rounds, the faint sounds of people beginning their daily routines in the apartments overhead.

"That said," Mien added with a grin that

showed just a hint of her needle-sharp teeth, "I wouldn't say no to grabbing a drink sometime. After everything we've been through, I think we've earned the right to call ourselves friends, don't you?"

"Definitely," Lianne replied, surprised by how much she meant it.

"Deal." Mien pushed herself away from the wall where she'd been leaning, her movements graceful despite the exhaustion that clung to her. For a moment, it looked as though she was about to head off in the opposite direction, their short alliance concluded with a genuinely pleasant separation that was rare in Lianne's line of work.

Then she stopped, turning back with an expression that suggested a sudden flash of inspiration.

"Actually," she said, "before we part ways, there's something I'd like to do. A parting gift, if you'll allow it." Her voice took on a formal quality, as though she were invoking some ancient custom or tradition that carried significance beyond simple courtesy. "I'd be honoured to enchant one of your weapons, so that something of my strength will always remain with you in spirit when you're next in battle."

The offer caught Lianne completely off guard, touching something deeper than professional respect or casual friendship. The gesture felt intimate, substantial in ways that went beyond mere practicality. "Mien, I..." she began, then stopped, deeply moved by the unexpected generosity. "That's incredibly kind of you. Are you sure?"

"Wholeheartedly," the banshee replied, her expression serious despite the warmth in her voice. "After what we've accomplished tonight, after what you've done for me, it's the least I can do. Besides, something tells me you're going to need all the help you can get in the future. Your reputation is only going to grow, and that will mean having to face increasingly dangerous opponents."

Lianne considered the weapons at her disposal, mentally running through her inventory of blades, stakes, and other tools of the trade. Each had its purpose, its place in her carefully organised arsenal, but one stood out as both practical and symbolic.

She drew her sword. It had served her faithfully on countless occasions. If any of her tools deserved enchantment, it was this one.

"This," she said, offering the blade to Mien handle-first. "It's never let me down."

Mien accepted the weapon with reverence. Her fingers traced the handle with surprising familiarity, as if she could read the intentions and hopes that had been forged into the material.

"Beautiful work," she murmured appreciatively. "The weaponsmith who made this understood their craft." She looked up, meeting Lianne's eyes with an intensity that made the air around them seem to thicken. "Are you ready?"

Lianne nodded, unsure of what to expect but trusting the banshee completely despite the brevity of their acquaintance.

What followed was unexpectedly quiet, a stark contrast to the overwhelming displays of power Lianne had witnessed throughout the night. Mien closed her eyes and brought the sword close to her body, holding it with both hands as if cradling something precious and fragile. Her lips moved silently, forming words in a language that predated human civilisation, syllables that seemed to resonate with frequencies beyond normal hearing.

The enchantment was subtle at first – a faint warmth emanating from the blade, barely perceptible. But gradually, the weapon began to glow with the same ethereal light that had surrounded the banshee during combat, a cold illumination that suggested power drawn from realms where death and life existed in perfect balance.

The light pulsed gently, in rhythm with something that might have been Mien's heartbeat or the cosmic rhythm of forces far greater than either of them. Ancient words continued to flow from her lips, each syllable charged with intent and purpose, weaving supernatural energy into the molecular structure of the blade itself.

When the glow stabilised, settling into the metal like captured moonlight, Mien opened her eyes and offered the weapon back to Lianne. The blade now radiated a soft, persistent luminescence with a reddish-orange hue that seemed to pulse with its own inner life, beautiful and deadly in equal measure.

"There," she said simply, though the effort had clearly drained her. Her ethereal glow had dimmed noticeably, as if she'd invested part of her essential nature into the enchantment. "It will serve you well, I think. The blade now carries something of what I am – the voice of death, the herald of endings. It will cut through supernatural defences that might otherwise turn aside conventional weapons, and it will never fail to find its mark when justice demands it."

With a slight tremble in her hands, Lianne accepted the weapon, overwhelmed by the magnitude of the gift. It felt different now – not heavier, but more present, as if it had acquired a consciousness of its own that recognised her as its wielder. The gentle glow was hypnotic, beautiful in a way that spoke of powers beyond human understanding.

"Mien, this is... I don't know how to thank you properly," she said, her voice thick with emotion she hadn't expected to feel. "This is extraordinary."

"Use it well," the banshee replied with a smile that carried traces of sadness alongside genuine affection. "Remember that every ending makes way for a new beginning, every death creates space for new life. That's what we fought for tonight – not just vengeance, but the opportunity for something better to grow in the absence of evil."

The moment stretched between them, heavy with significance and unspoken understanding. They had shared violence and vulnerability, fought side by side against supernatural forces that would have overwhelmed either of them alone. In the short period of time they had known each other, they had become something more than allies or professional associates – they had truly become friends, bound by battle and mutual respect.

"This is goodbye, then," Mien said eventually, her voice carrying a finality that made the words feel like a formal conclusion to their partnership.

"For now," Lianne replied, not quite ready to accept that their paths might never cross again. "But I have a feeling this isn't the last time we'll see each other."

Mien's grin was sharp and brilliant, revealing the nature that lurked beneath her more unremarkable façade. "Me too."

With that, she turned and walked away down the alley, her footsteps making no sound on the wet pavement despite the solid reality of her presence. She moved like shadow made manifest, graceful and otherworldly, until she turned the corner and vanished from sight as completely as if she had never existed at all.

Lianne stood alone, holding her enchanted weapon and watching the space where the banshee had disappeared. The glow of her blade cast shifting patterns on the brick walls around her, and she could feel the weapon's new power humming against her palm like a living thing.

Carefully, reverently, she put the sword back into its sheath. The glow dimmed but didn't disappear entirely, becoming a subtle luminescence that would probably be invisible to anyone who wasn't looking for it.

She found herself smiling as she reflected on the night's events and the unlikely partnership that had made them possible. Working with

Mien had been challenging, dangerous, and ultimately rewarding in ways that went beyond simple professional satisfaction. The banshee had pushed her to think differently about her methods.

But she was also relieved to be returning to solo work, to the familiar rhythms of individual hunting that had sustained her for a decade. Partnerships brought complications – divided attention, emotional investment, the constant need to co-ordinate and communicate under pressure. Working alone meant freedom, self-reliance, the ability to make split-second decisions without consulting anyone else.

The rising sun painted the alley in shades of gold and amber that transformed the urban decay into something almost beautiful. Somewhere in the distance, she could hear the city fully awakening – traffic building to its daily crescendo, shop owners opening their doors, the eternal human symphony of life continuing despite the paranormal drama that had played out in its shadows.

She adjusted her gear, checked her weapons, and began walking through the maze of alleyways in the direction of home. Her phone would probably start ringing soon – it always did after word got out about successful hunts. Wealthy clients who had heard whispers about her work, desperate people facing supernatural problems they couldn't solve through conventional means, law enforcement officials who needed someone to handle the cases that didn't fit into normal categories.

The thought filled her with anticipation rather than dread. She was good at what she did – exceptional, even – and now she had an enchanted weapon that would make her even more effective against supernatural threats. Whatever came next – whether a common nuisance or something particularly sadistic with delusions of grandeur – she would be ready.

For a price, of course. She was a professional, after all, and professionals got paid for their expertise.

After all, she was Lianne Cross, demon hunter extraordinaire, and business was good.

www.ingramcontent.com/pod-product-compliance
Lightning Source LLC
Chambersburg PA
CBHW032019180726
48283CB00008B/2742